T0199012

THE GOURD OF WISDOM

Olubunmi Salako

© 2020 Olubunmi Salako. All rights reserved.

No part of this book may be reproduced, stored in a retrieval system, or transmitted
by any means without the written permission of the author.

AuthorHouse™ UK
1663 Liberty Drive
Bloomington, IN 47403 USA
www.authorhouse.co.uk
UK TFN: 0800 0148641 (Toll Free inside the UK)
UK Local: 02036 956322 (+44 20 3695 6322 from outside the UK)

Because of the dynamic nature of the Internet, any web addresses or links contained in this book may have changed since publication and may no longer be valid. The views expressed in this work are solely those of the author and do not necessarily reflect the views of the publisher, and the publisher hereby disclaims any responsibility for them.

Any people depicted in stock imagery provided by Getty Images are models,
and such images are being used for illustrative purposes only.
Certain stock imagery © Getty Images.

This book is printed on acid-free paper.

ISBN: 978-1-7283-5425-5 (sc)
ISBN: 978-1-7283-5424-8 (e)

Print information available on the last page.

Published by AuthorHouse 06/19/2020

authorHOUSE®

Long, long ago in the animal kingdom, the Tortoise had many friends and was famous for his wisdom. King Lion always called him for advice whenever he wanted to take an important decision. Other animals also came to him for help when they had problems.

The animals respected him for his wisdom and he enjoyed this enviable position. On the other hand, he was a lazy animal that relied on others to feed.

He regularly got rewarded for his wisdom. He got meat from the Lion anytime he returned from hunting. Some animals would give him pawpaw, oranges and apples while others gave him lettuce, spinach and cucumber.

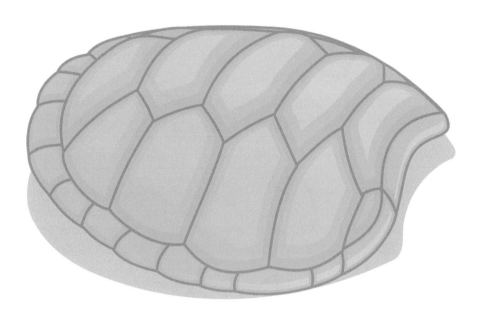

This was how he lived. He had no farm of his own and he lived in his shell which he carried with him everywhere he went. He was afraid to lose his source of daily meals.

He would give anything to retain this important position.

One day, King Lion called all the animals for a meeting to discuss about their safety in the kingdom. Many hunters came to the forest to kill the animals.

"What can we do to stop the killings by the hunters?" King Lion asked.

Chimpanzee spoke first.

"We must put a team together and give them roles to play to secure the forest."

King Lion was happy with his suggestion. He nodded in agreement. All the animals supported the idea.

King Lion asked for volunteers who would work in the team.

Some of the animals showed interest with a raise of hand. King Lion chose Rat, Dog, Pigeon, Raven, pig, Elephant, Cow, Duck, Bee, and Squirrel.

These animals are considered some of the smartest in the forest.

Tortoise was lost for words. He did not believe that Chimpanzee could come up with such a brilliant idea.

He paced up and down, thinking of what to say.

"That's a good suggestion," he giggled.

He left shortly after feeling very worried.

Tortoise became afraid of losing his position. He became very nervous at the thought. He must stop this from happening. He thought about this for many days and came up with a plot.

Tortoise always had solutions to problems, but he got it all wrong this time.

"I will collect all the wisdom in the kingdom and store it in a big gourd and keep it," he said.

"I must remain the wisest animal in this kingdom," he said to himself.

The next day, he got a very big gourd and visited all the animals who volunteered to work for the king.

He listened to how they planned to carry out the assignment. One after the other, he put their wisdom in his big gourd.

It took him several days to do this. Remember, Tortoise is a very slow animal. He went everywhere to make sure none was left.

He was very pleased with himself.

"I must now keep this gourd in a secret place away from everyone," he asserted

"But where shall I keep it?" he thought to himself.

He decided to keep it on a very tall tree. He then located the tallest tree in the forest.

He intended to live under the tree so no one would get access to the gourd.

The next day, he got up very early. He walked for many hours dragging his gourd of wisdom along.

He got to the tree just before the other animals woke up. He looked around to ensure no one was watching him.

He took out the rope he had kept in the gourd, tied it at the neck of the gourd, and put it around his own neck with the gourd of wisdom in front of him.

He tried to climb the tree, but it was difficult.

Each time he tried, he failed. The gourd got in his way.

He tried many times, and failed. Soon he got so tired and felt very angry with himself.

He decided to rest and think of what to do.

Soon it was daylight, other animals were up and about.

It was the cunning Fox who first saw him on the way to his farm.

"What are you doing here so early?" he asked Tortoise.

"I'm trying to climb the tree to get some herbs for my wife," he lied.

"Each time I tried, I failed and I am very tired," he explained.

"Try again and let me see," Fox instructed.

Tortoise got up and tried again with the gourd in front of him. Again the gourd got in his way.

I thought you are a wise animal, Fox laughed sarcastically.

He laughed and laughed.

Tortoise became really angry wondering why Fox was laughing at him.

"Why are you laughing?" he asked angrily.

"I am laughing because you are very foolish," answered Fox.

Tortoise was shocked at this statement.

The word, foolish was strange in Tortoise's ears. He was known to be wise.

"You will never be able to climb the tree with the gourd in front of you," said the Fox.

"Put the gourd behind you and try again."

Tortoise placed the gourd of wisdom at his back. Now he could climb the tree easily.

Tortoise was ashamed of himself. He knew Fox will tell all his friends.

Fox left him and went on his way.

Tortoise was happy thinking his plan had worked. He sang as he climbed on.

Suddenly he realized he could not have collected all the wisdom in the kingdom. The advice Fox gave him made sense.

He knew without a doubt that Fox was also wise.

He was convinced that he had not collected all the wisdom in the kingdom. He realised it was impossible to collect all the wisdom and keep to himself.

He was very disappointed and irritated. He angrily threw down the gourd of wisdom.

The gourd shattered into pieces as soon as it landed on a nearby rock.

Tortoise decided to join the team of animals working for the safety in the forest.

He learnt a good lesson that no one knows it all.

We need to learn from each other to build our experiences and acquire wisdom. We must also be happy to share our knowledge with others and not be selfish.

Printed in the United States
By Bookmasters